to the girl who would write poems in her journal, and dream of the life she is living now. all of your work is here for everyone to enjoy, you never thought we would get this far.
to my younger self, who i owe my success to, this is a reminder.

we were never loveless.

the beach seems to be,
an illusion of some sort.
i see it in my dreams most nights.

i recall getting lost in the sand.
dreaming about the earth,
and how it swallowed me whole.

almost as if the core of the planet,
weeped for me and said,
i have been gone for too long.

i return to reality, rudely awaken;
reckless and ruined, by my own doings.

we destroy the ones we love,
and rip flowers from their home.
we encase them in glass,
where they don't belong.

we ignore the ones we love,
in an attempt to get their attention.
we wear sadness as attire
and beg for affection.

we fall in love with the ones,
we know aren't good for us.
but cry when it ends,
we knew they couldn't love us.

we must learn to become our protection.
as of now, we're the reason for our destruction.

self sabotage

she fell in love, but not with a person.
she fell in love with the way her mind worked.
she fell in love with the color yellow, and the sun and
moon's tragic love story.
she fell in love with the painting that sparked her soul, and
made her feel something.
she fell in love with the roses in the garden, and the strong
women who guarded them.

fallen from the cliff of hope, i hung onto one last thread.
the things we long for are what destroys us in the end.

sunken into the deep abyss, sadness had overtaken me.
i had barely recognized myself.
a complete stranger staring back, is this who i've become?

i once was told that the only way out was through.
feel your pain, mend your soul.
but the deep sting of the loss of you, became numbing.

i gave into the river, the current was too harsh.
i had no fight left in me, my faith disappeared.
i now stare at the cliff, with an ache in my heart,
wishing i were still there.

it's 7pm and the coffee pot sings.
to my mother, it eases her worries.
she sips with shaky hands,
her tired eyes a permanent stare.

it's 12am and the coffee is cold.
to my grandmother, she craves it.
the feeling of being alive,
after exhaustion becomes her being.

they speak of life and their trials.
love that has gone wrong,
and the pieces of their heart,
that they find within the pot.

i take a deep breathe,
looking back at the trials i've faced.
tired eyes and sad smiles fade,
as the coffee is done being made.

if you ever feel as if you're failing.
and the world seems too challenging,
remember you're made of stars;
all sparkling and broken.

an excerpt from a story i'll never write

just like that she was off, the pitter patter of her heel the last memory i have of us. she was off, to a better place, to better her-self, and to find a man who could love her in all the ways i refused to.
when it's all over, it's so easy to blame love for it ending terribly. but love was always there. love was there at the edge of my bed, when i sat there, head in hands, praying i could change. love was there in the back of her car when she gripped the steering wheel tight, on the night i couldn't put aside my pride. the night her bright smile and childlike eyes turned cold. the night i knew, in my heart, i had to let her go.

the only thing i was certain of was that it wasn't love's fault, it was mine.
love wanted it to end differently, too.

the world seemed so far above me, drowning in the waves,
gasping for air.
i'm met with the blinding sun.
the sun i once adored, now the thing to bury me.

connected to my heart, i see chains, locked onto the cosmos,
leading back to you.
the moon returns, i take a breath, gasping for love and sweet affec-
tions.
the moonlight kisses my skin, as i lay there weary,
fearing the sun will return again.

it was sad, really, the only time she experienced true
emotion was within ink,
and people who weren't real.

if i hate you, it'll be easy.
it'll be easy to leave.
it'll be easy to make you understand,
that you deserve more than me.

if i hate you, i wouldn't care.
i wouldn't care that i made you mad.
i wouldn't want you to change.
but i don't hate you. i love you more than anything.

if i never met you, i would be lost.
lost without a home, or a shoulder to cry on.
i wouldn't kiss your forehead, and you lay on my chest.
and i would have never experienced peaceful bliss.

being a writer means to bleed every heartbreaking experience you've had, you must reach into the darkest parts of yourself and allow it to destroy you.

in this lifetime,
it's impossible to love.
in this state of mind,
it's meaning we're deprived of.

if we think of ourselves as colors,
i'm ashamed to say i'm blue.
but aren't all lovers?

i aspire to be red,
with their invincible souls.
and how they're so passionate,
no doubt they are fully whole.

i have missing pieces of me,
that i've yet to find.
we choose who we are,
it's all in our mind.

mindset

your eyes were the color of the heavens above.
when i thought about being in love,
i never pictured tired eyes, or telling myself lies.
i never fathomed late nights or total flight.
i thought about roses and dancing with no music.
i thought about how bad it hurts to lose it.

there's something that always brings me back to him,
his philosophy is strictly forbidden.
but it doesn't seem all that bad to lose everything,
curious of what the unknown will bring.
words kept spewing out of me,
like a river only certain souls would believe.

nonetheless, i denied it over and over.
they tell me i'll understand when i'm older,
i don't care about years from now.
i just need to know how, one soul can take a toll on me.
you make me forfeit the strength i keep.

my hands shake from all the emotion passing through,
all i write, the page becomes of you.
maybe we aren't meant to be and that's okay.
just know that it hurts to turn away.

there's shattered glass on the windowsill,
memories i can't ever manage.
the sadness we attempt to kill,
lurks to our disadvantage.
with shaky hands and shortened breath,
why do we continue to love the people who have left?

an excerpt from a story i'll never write

"don't be scared," he tried to soothe but the fire of her soul won't rest.

"how? how can't I be?"

his eyes fell upon the stained wood, paint embroidered itself into it, rightfully claiming that his home will always be made up of art.

"i don't want to hurt you."

"no. you don't. but you will." he noticed the shakiness in her voice, the silent tremble that she would never allow him to encounter but he saw right through her.

 she was always a little too strong for her own good. god forbid she began to need someone, to see the good in them, to start to believe in them.

she thought it made her vulnerable. he thought it defined her.

"i swear i won't. your idea of love is far from the truth," he said. he knew her tactics, how she would run away from any emotion that wasn't anger. how she hates that fuzzy feeling her stomach.

she stood silent.

"you think about the ending of everything. your initial reaction is to think of the worst." he silently said, as she couldn't tear her eyes away from her shoes.

"you know what I'm scared of? i'm scared of discovering safety in your eyes and being forced to stare into them when it's all over, when you tell me I was a mistake, that you shouldn't have let me get so attached to you."

"I would nev-"

"i'm terrified of dry heaving on a cold bathroom floor because you found someone better or clutching a tear stained pillow pretending it's you. i'm terrified of losing you."

he wouldn't be able to get through to her. she was broken long before he began to know her ruthless soul.

"so it's better to never have me? is this what you're saying?"

she nodded as if pondering over the question herself.

all the drawings he sketched of her, the paintings he spent hours and hours on, studying her features whilst planning on carving her

into the mountains for the entire world to encounter.
she is made up of fire,water, anger and sadness. the entire world
was carefully crafted into her eyes.
the eyes he fell deeply in love with.
the eyes he may never even see again.
she picked up her bag, took one last look at the room, trembled
some more, and then left.
he only hoped she would change her mind.

we express ourselves through ink and scribbled minds,
longing for meaning we may never find.
we hold our heads high and project our voices,
in a failed attempt to never regret our choices.

in the universe i was a curse,
lurking wherever they brought me.
behind written bars, with all of these scars,
i just want to be freed.

just know loving him will not be easy,
he'll hand you the bullets and beg you to pull the trigger.

"i would die for you," he said.
"live for me, that's even harder," i replied.

how many times have we been here before?
how many fights can our hearts endure?
how many nights will i spend on the floor?
how many, until we're no more?

i can't say i hate who i am, when i'm with you.
and i can't say i hate who i've become, because of you.

ode to my first heartbreak.

i recall you saying there were forty one girls before me, that's forty
one hearts that had been broken by you.
i'm ashamed to say i'm number forty two.
your heart's exterior had been damaged before, that's not an excuse
to hurt anyone else.
i recall you telling me you hate yourself, for all the karma headed
your way.
that was before you drifted off to slumber and denied it all the
next day.
you broke my heart impulsively and pinned my pain on me, you
said you did that because i was "toxic"
because toxic people make sure you eat everyday, huh?
toxic people listen to you cry yourself to sleep, and toxic people
reassure you whenever you need it?
no one stood for too long and you know that eats you up. i was
toxic to your soul because i wanted your love and someone as selfish as you refused to give it up.
i told you things about me no one else knew. and i bet you keep
all your lover's secrets in a jar, under your bed near your guitar. the
same guitar you played while i fell asleep, whispering promises you
knew you'd never keep.
you said you wanted to protect me from all the bad in the world.
the only bad in my world was the lies you told and your heart that
was ice cold.
you say you're tired of hurting people and i say i'm tired of
being hurt.
everything seemed to work.
until the day you shut it all down. when all my thoughts contained
you and everything hurt.
i swore that heartbreak could never be worse.
and that's why i'm so glad you were my first.

i don't need you.
i don't need your approval, or criticism.
i don't need your constant nagging, or lack of affection.
i don't need someone who puts me down, when i'm mountains
above the clouds.
i don't need you to tell me what i'm capable of.
i don't need you to break my spirit, like you always have.
so go ahead, leave like the ones before.
i don't need this unnecessary pain.
or love that is in vain.

if we ever parted, would i be the first thing on your mind,
when you wake up from those long nights?
would you think of my hands, that used to stroke your hair,
in the morning sunlight?

would you think of me when your eyes open?
and when you turn over and see the empty space,
i used to lay, dreaming of lavender fields and peace.

would you mourn my presence?
would you think of all the wrongs in our love?
would your world come to a halt, as i fade from your existence?

if we ever parted, the sea would stand still.
the clouds would cry for your return.
the stars, reminders of wishes not granted.
parting from my other half, would make me feel incomplete.
but would my other half feel as i did, if we ever parted?

she felt as if she were drifting through time and space,
deciphering nursery rhymes and lullabies.
thinking of who would eventually take her place,
the one to make art far better than her limited mind.
the one who thinks the stars are the antidote,
for the world's sadness.
the one who will never have to say, they almost had it.
she picks up a pen like it's a weapon.
she scribbles ink on each and every person she lets in.
they tell her she's brave for using her voice,
her response is the same, she never had a choice.
she needed them to know, her existence was never rehearsed.
she is far more than the pink stitches her mother used to sew.
she is the entire universe.

breathing seems like too much of a challenge.
my heart is heavy as i smile at the sky,
with tear filled eyes and a broken spirit.
my chest hurts and i can't go on further.

look at the birds, he said. everything will be great.
nothing made sense from that moment on,
how can you come into my life and change me?

i know it's not your fault for being who you are,
but it's my fault for falling in love with you.
while i dream of you, you dream of her.
and history repeats itself, because my skin hasn't shed.

i want to change to be more poetic.
it's hard when i'm afraid of judgment.
i guess that's why you love her,
because she's everything i'm not.

my heart is broken, on the floor near your shoe.
you look down at it and weep.
i know you didn't mean it.

when those words were spoken, i saw something new.
a spark of hope in your eyes,
for the girl i know you wish to pursue.

although i am hurting, and i'm mourning.
i need you to look the other way.
i'll dry my tears and smile anyways.

i can't let you know i'm hurting,
because then it'll hurt you.
i know everything happens for a reason,
what the reason is, i have no clue.

i trust my angels,
they brought me to you.
no matter how many tears i shed,
i'll always be thankful for the time i had a piece of you.

i'm fighting for us, against you.
please, meet me in the middle.

you deserve so much more than what you've settled for.
you deserve a booming, unconditional, fiery love.

how pathetic she felt, begging for love for a man,
who wasn't capable of doing so.

right now i feel heavy, my heart is sinking down to my stomach, slowly but surely deteriorating with each breath I take.
i don't know why this hurts, i don't like how it does. the world seems to be at a standpoint, or maybe i'm at a standpoint and I can't keep up with life around me.

i love him, i love him so much that i don't know what to do.
birds have to fly and just because my wings are clipped, doesn't mean his should be too.
but i want him to stay with me, in the eye of the hurricane, never changing, always staying the same. i do not want to be changed, i don't want to accept it.

i want to feel wanted, like i'm the only person in the universe who can make him happy. i've been everything but that lately. i know i'm not easy.
i only hope i can be his peace someday.

how naive can we be?
wishing on dandelions and stars.
we must stop trying to change who we are.

you cannot change the battles you've faced.
learn to accept it, smile and say thank you.
it's made you a warrior.

we are all equal,
in the eyes of monsters,
we are divided.
by color,
by belief,
by gender,
by choices of love,
unity will bring us closer.
fighting for freedom,
an unstoppable force we become,
when we join as one.

please don't fear the broken road,
the one with numerous pot holes.
the one with unlucky outcomes,
and broken hearts.
the universe has a plan,
and is ever changing.
as if this life won't have a happy ending.

this city depicts hope, in its purest form.
living streets where dreams are born.
don't fall into it's twisted ways,
don't let the world fade to gray.

rain falls down over the city,
kaleidoscopic flashbacks of who we were burden me.
we've seemed to put our old selves in a frame,
never to be touched again.
i still feel the night, and illumination of the stars,
even now that we're miles apart.

walls separate us, but we cry it's unfair.
we are doing nothing to change it,
like we don't even care.
we scream at each other to open up,
and blame each other for what we could have done.
but dare to hate what we've become.

in the dark of night, when the sun hides away.
when the moon shines bright, i beg that you stay.
i stare at the ceiling, counting the tiles,
clutching my journal to my chest.
you tell me there are so many trials,
because of all that you suppress.
from the moment i met you,
i wanted to know everything.
before you came around, i was scared to love.
but my walls were broken down.
how do i explain your soul,
to the others who just don't understand?
all i know is that they were right,
when they say the best things in life are unplanned.

i have so many thoughts, all racing and complex.
so many emotions that endlessly run through my head.

feelings are meant to be felt, however intense.
never be ashamed of the heart hidden behind your breast.

love and learn, so many stories i've told.
the ones of pain and seashells, near wavering waters.

you live and learn.

i want to keep you here in this moment.
the moments where your heart is fully available to me.
i want to freeze your sweet words and forget the cold ones.
i want to stay here, in this bed, while you clutch onto me,
like i'm the only thing you ever need.
i want to feel your heart, in all it's beauty.
like a blooming flower within the winter months.

i keep you here, in my mind.
we never leave these sheets and you never make me cry.
i'm reality stricken once again,
when i feel the emptiness in our bed.

hostage

the winter months became my solitude.
the fireplace warming your cold heart.
the world is different than it was when we were kids.
if only those kids knew what they were in for.

i feel like a child again, when in your embrace.
when you smile, i get sent back to years before.
the years we pranced around in the december snow,
when your heart was full and warm.
when the world was endless with possibilities,
and we were excited to live.

i wish these winter months could warm you up,
like it once did.

she possesses the same tired eyes as my mother,
eyes that look defeated and worn.
how strong she was, i never knew,
when i was young, i was so unforgiving.

she fought day and night to stay afloat,
all while trying to care for her kin.
the love she had, was never seen,
but felt just like the wind.

mother

the clouds collect your tears,
as you watch over the ones left behind.

you were so strong in those final moments.
the release of life arrived sooner than expected,
although i wish you stayed, the angels needed you.

how selfish i thought they were, to take you from me.
i never knew they felt the loss of you all these years.
they set you free to live a beautiful life,
mourning your absence.

i share your presence with those angels,
they show you to me.
how angry i was for their selfishness,
revealed the reflection of me.

the angels loved you dearly and needed you to come home.
they were so brave to let you leave for so long.

i forgive you, angels.

i forgive you,
even though i know you're not sorry.

i shouldn't ask why you're sad,
when the skies are gray.
i should know by now,
the universe is in sync with your being.

an excerpt from a story i'll never write.

his words came out almost inaudible, he was struggling to find the right thing to say, she just needed to hear one last thing.
"i remember the first day i saw you, you were so beautiful. and i remember that it hurt because you would never be mine to keep." he spoke softly. her silent tears came pouring through, his grip loosened. she wanted to scream.
he needed to hold on, he was the one who taught her what love was supposed to be.
"when you told me you loved me, i knew then i could die happily. you're the one thing in this world that made sense to me." he said.
he was art. he was this angelic, torturous, heart shattering canvas that she wished she spent more time painting, perfecting. he was the pain, the love, the method to the madness.
he was the happiest and saddest parts of her.
"i'm sorry i couldn't live for you." those were the last words he would ever speak.
the defeating sound echoed throughout the room.
she buried her head into his chest, sobbing uncontrollably, as the memories of them played in her head.
as she laid there, broken hearted and tired, she swore she could still hear his heartbeat.

night speaks to me,
fall in love or fall apart.
nobody is there to know,
which you choose.

i lay awake uncertain,
tears pouring from my eyes,
wishing on illuminate light,
in the night sky.

cold air and summer scent,
remind me of sadness.
it reminds me of the nights,
i wish to be okay again.

when the star burns out,
the wish had been granted,
and the wisher is fulfilled.

so i chose my star
and made my wish.
it has been months since that day.

i've seen others get what they asked for,
all happy and teary eyed.
they say my time will come.

i waited and waited but to my dismay,
my star is still the brightest one.

i think i went wrong when i only wanted to better for you,
i need to want to be better for myself.

i wish i knew you then,
when your eyes lit up and you swore you could touch the stars.
when childhood dreams seemed so in reach,
when your love was pure and your heart was full.

i wish i cherished the love you had,
when everything was new and promising.
i wish i was kind to you although my heart was cold.

you deserved so much more than i gave you.

your eyes are poison to my ambition.
my desires fade away when you're near.
the view of my dreams disappear.
as if you're the cure to my sadness,
the world never made sense before you.
leaving me gasping for air, clinging onto strings,
trying to remain the person you fell in love with.

she realized her battle was with the world and its lack of meaning. those storybook characters would never face the challenges she had. her mr.darcy wasn't a proud man, he was the boy who made eye contact with her in the hallway. although she was elizabeth, so strong and wise. her wisdom was far beyond her years. her wisdom meant so little to people around her. she never got the storybook love. she got the one sided love.

she wrote love letters and poems, carrying hope that one day he'd do the same for her.

she dreamt of love and the big city, pouring her heart into the pages of her journal, swearing he was the one.

but he wasn't, he didn't deserve the love she had for him.

i am in constant fear that i'm doing the wrong thing.

you are what i wish home felt like.

in this closing,
if you take anything from these pages, let it be this- you are worthy
of love. you deserve happiness. don't let your mind fool you.

i am so proud of you for never giving up.
thank you for being who you are.

love,
chanteli.

Made in United States
North Haven, CT
03 February 2024

48182950R10039